8/08

THE SECRET
Olivia Told Me

by N. Joy

illustrations by
Nancy Devard

Published by Just Us Books, Inc.
356 Glenwood Avenue, East Orange, NJ 07017
www.justusbooks.com
ISBN: 978-1-933491-08-0
Printed in the USA
10 9 8 7 6 5 4 3 2
Cataloging in Publication Data is available.

To my son, Randy "Ran-Ran" Erby,
the person I wrote this story with when he was only four years old.
I'm blessed now to share it with the world.
—N. J.

To my nieces and nephews and the Moore children
for their profiles and inspiration,
and to CompRecovery for fixing the unfixable.
—N. D.

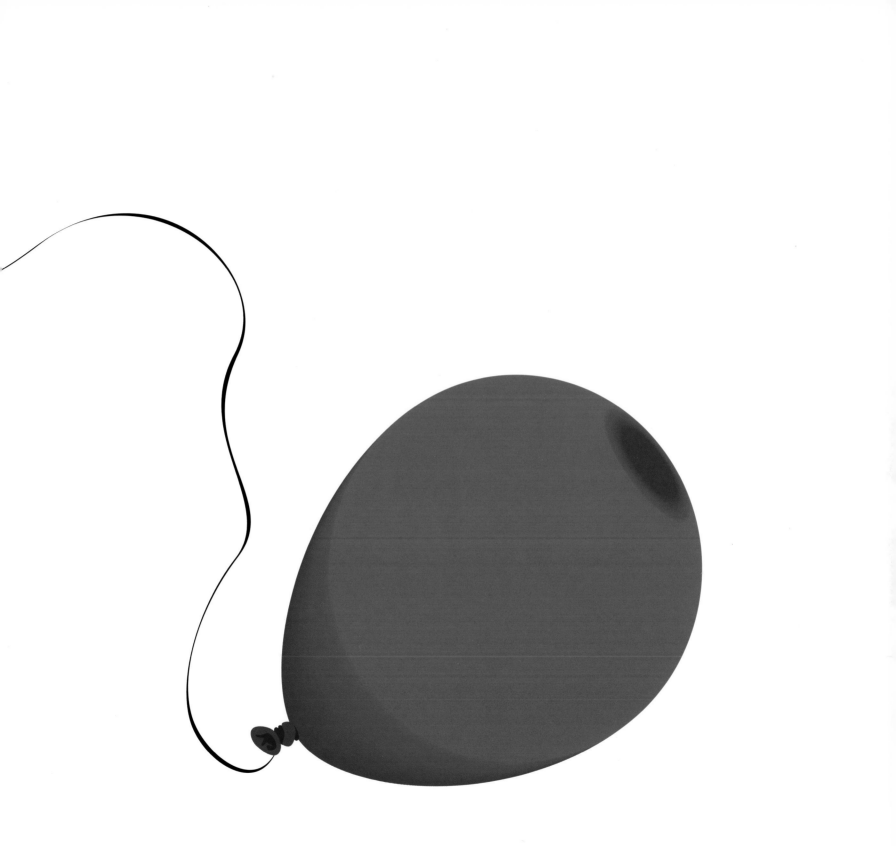

Olivia told me a **SECRET.**

I promised I would not tell.

It was such a great, **big** secret,
I thought my head might swell.

It was hard not to tell the secret.
I wanted to spread the news.

But I gave Olivia my word.
Her friendship I could not lose.

As I played with my classmate, Ayanna,
the secret accidentally slipped.

Before I could catch the secret,
it tumbled right out of my lips.

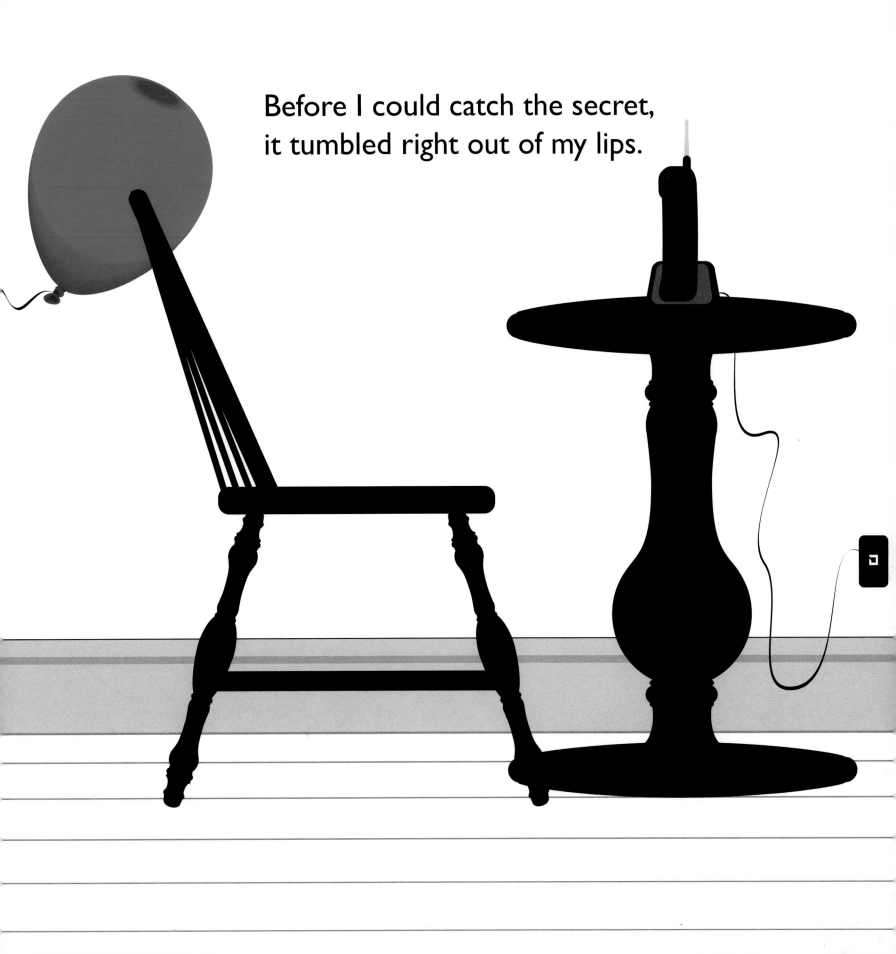

Ayanna chatted with Stephanie.
And at once Stephanie knew.

Then Steph whispered to Tony.
She declared that it was **true**.

Tony leaked the secret to Jalen.
Jalen's sister, Anita, overheard.

It didn't take long for Anita
to start spreading the word.

Anita told her friend, Terri.
To the secret she added more.

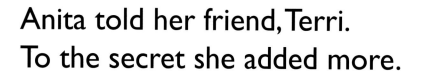

When Terri told Tabby the secret,
it was **bigger** than ever before.

Tabby passed it on to her classmates.
She blew up the secret, too.

More and more people told the secret
and it **grew** and **grew** and **grew**.

The secret became even **bigger**,
with parts that were not true.

The secret was no longer special
because now **everyone** knew.

I thought and
I worried
and I fretted.

What *did* I get myself into?

So I decided to tell Olivia the truth,
'cause it was the right
thing to do.

"I'm sorry," I said to Olivia.
"You *know* I am your friend."

"I made a mistake. The secret is out.
**Please don't let our friendship
end!"**

Together we both learned a lesson.
Of this we're very sure.

"Don't tell a **single** person a secret.
Or it won't be a secret **anymore!**"

AUTHOR'S NOTE

In this story, Olivia has a secret that she shares with her friend. Has anyone ever asked you to keep a secret?

Did you keep it? Why?
Or why not?

What do you think Olivia's secret might have been?

Do you have any secrets that you've shared with others?

Did they tell the secret (like Olivia's friend did) or did they keep it?

Why do you think people keep secrets?

Why do you think it's hard for people *not* to tell secrets?

Are there any secrets that you shouldn't keep?

Was the final decision Olivia's friend made a good one?
Why or why not?

About the Author

N. Joy writes children's and young adult books as well as urban Christian fiction for adults. The executive editor for a new Christian imprint and a magazine columnist, she is currently working on a young adult series entitled *The Soul Sisters*. N. Joy's writing is also featured in an African American greeting card box set. N. Joy lives in the Midwest with her husband and three children.

About the Illustrator

Nancy Devard is a former engineer turned professional artist. After earning a Bachelor of Science from Temple University, and working as a Development Engineer, she decided to pursue her passion—fine art and illustration. Devard worked as staff artist for Hallmark Cards, creating best-selling designs for the Mahogany and Kids divisions. As a freelance illustrator, she says, "My thrill comes when I look at the work I've completed and feel a sense of satisfaction." *The Secret Olivia Told Me* is her first trade picture book with Just Us Books. It was named a 2008 Coretta Scott King Honor Award for illustration by the American Library Association.

This book was typeset in Gills Sans.
The illustrations were first sketched in pencil, then created electronically using Adobe Illustrator.

Just Us Books, Inc.
Premier Publisher of Black—Interest Books for Young People
356 Glenwood Avenue
East Orange, NJ 07017

visit us at
www.justusbooks.com